LEARNS TO FLY!

BY **KARA WEST**   ILLUSTRATED BY **LEEZA HERNANDEZ**

LITTLE SIMON

New York London Toronto Sydney New Delhi

LITTLE SIMON
An imprint of Simon & Schuster Children's Publishing Division
1230 Avenue of the Americas, New York, New York 10020
First Little Simon paperback edition December 2018
Copyright © 2018 by Simon & Schuster, Inc.
Also available in a Little Simon hardcover edition
All rights reserved, including the right of reproduction in whole or in part in any form.
LITTLE SIMON is a registered trademark of Simon & Schuster, Inc., and associated colophon is a trademark of Simon & Schuster, Inc.
For information about special discounts for bulk purchases, please contact Simon & Schuster Special Sales at 1-866-506-1949 or business@simonandschuster.com.
The Simon & Schuster Speakers Bureau can bring authors to your live event. For more information or to book an event contact the Simon & Schuster Speakers Bureau at 1-866-248-3049 or visit our website at www.simonspeakers.com.
Designed by Laura Roode
Manufactured in the United States of America 0919 MTN
4 6 8 10 9 7 5 3
Library of Congress Cataloging-in-Publication Data
Names: West, Kara, author. | Hernandez, Leeza, illustrator.
Title: Mia Mayhem learns to fly! / by Kara West ; illustrated by Leeza Hernandez.
Description: First Little Simon paperback edition. | New York : Little Simon, 2018. | Series: Mia Mayhem ; 2 | Summary: "With help from her best friend and the super academy's most talented flier, Mia learns how to fly!"—Provided by publisher.
Identifiers: LCCN 2018038756 (paperback) | ISBN 9781534432727 (paperback) | ISBN 9781534432734 (hc) | ISBN 9781534432741 (eBook) | Subjects: | CYAC: Superheroes—Fiction. | Flight—Fiction. | Dogs—Fiction. | Cats—Fiction. | African Americans—Fiction. | BISAC: JUVENILE FICTION / Action & Adventure / General. | JUVENILE FICTION / Readers / Chapter Books.
Classification: LCC PZ7.1.W43684 Ml 2018 | DDC [E]—dc23
LC record available at https://lccn.loc.gov/2018038756

CONTENTS

CHAPTER 1   IN THE DOGHOUSE   1

CHAPTER 2   THE WIND TUNNEL   17

CHAPTER 3   PAWSITIVELY HEROIC   29

CHAPTER 4   THE NEW MISSION   39

CHAPTER 5   CHAOS IN THE COMPASS   49

CHAPTER 6   THE TEAM GETS BIGGER   57

CHAPTER 7   FLYING! OR . . . SORT OF   69

CHAPTER 8   EDDIE'S WILD RIDE   85

CHAPTER 9   THE FINAL DESTINATION   91

CHAPTER 10   THE DREAM TEAM   103

IN THE
DOGHOUSE

Most cats like to lay in the sun or scratch at things or take naps.

But not *my* cat: Chaos is her name, and chaos is her game. On a typical afternoon, she'll excitedly zoom around the kitchen, knock over a honey bottle, and then land right in the middle of it.

And as you can see, that's exactly what just happened.

Chaos doesn't really *mean* to cause trouble. And I should know. I have a bit of a reputation for causing chaos and mayhem myself.

Oh, I should probably explain before I go on. Allow me to introduce myself. My name is Mia Macarooney.

During the day, I attend Normal Elementary School. But as soon as the school bell rings, I'm Mia Mayhem—the world's newest superhero!

For real. Yours truly has superpowers!

And guess what? I'm going to learn how to *fly*!

And that means when regular school ends, I head straight to the Program for In Training Superheroes aka the PITS! But today, my flying class was starting late, so I ran home to make a honey and peanut butter sandwich.

Sounds like a great idea, right?

I thought so too. But as you can see, things can get pretty sticky real fast if you have a curious cat like mine.

I may have superpowers, but cleaning a whole jar of honey off a crazy cat? That's a job for a professional.

So I rushed Chaos over to my dad's animal clinic.

He's really good with animals. And I don't just mean as a veterinarian.

Here's the deal: He's a superhero too! Both my parents are.

Just like me, my mom and dad lead ordinary lives in order to protect their secret identities. Most of the time, our lives are pretty quiet. But turns out today was not the best time for a vet visit. The office was busy because the Downtown Dog Palooza, our town's annual dog show, was tomorrow.

I nervously looked at the clock. I was going to be late for class. But luckily, my dad cleaned up Chaos in a flash.

I led my cat back into her carrier and sped out the door without looking back. I had to get to the PITS before the last bell.

Thankfully, I didn't have to go too far because the PITS building was right next to my regular school! All my life, I thought it was just an empty warehouse . . . but everything changed when I found out I was a *superhero*!

Turns out that this normal old warehouse is the coolest place *ever*! (But more on that later.)

When I arrived at the front entrance,
I grabbed my supersuit from my bag
and spun around.

This new quick-superhero-change
trick took *a lot* of practice. I held out

my hand to Chaos for a fist bump, but when I looked down . . . Chaos wasn't the only animal there!

There was a pack of dogs excitedly panting all around me. Somehow we'd been followed! I instantly regretted not making sure the door was closed after leaving the clinic.

I looked around nervously. There was only one I recognized—my best friend's dog, Pax.

WOOF! Pax jumped on me so hard that I fell back.

When I picked myself up, that's
when I heard it.

Someone was coming, and I had to
think fast . . . or we would all be seen!

I quickly straightened
the crooked DO NOT ENTER
sign—which opened
the secret entrance
to the PITS—and
scanned myself in.

As the door opened, Chaos pawed her way out of the carrier and raced into the building—with the pack of dogs right behind her!

Oh boy. I was in the doghouse now.

15

THE WIND TUNNEL

I chased after Chaos and the dogs into the main lobby. The center of the tall building, also known as the Compass, was bustling with superheroes. I thought that I'd get in trouble for bringing in a pack of loose animals, but no one stopped us!

I think that's because everyone here has seen weirder things.

The PITS is a top secret superhero-training academy that offers classes in every super-skill, from flying to foreign languages. (That's the class where you learn how to talk to animals.)

And look—I almost crashed into someone who was shooting heat lasers into a wall. This place is the coolest!

So I guess seeing a pack of adorable dogs chasing a speedy cat is . . . actually normal.

When I finally got to Professor Wingum's flying class, he didn't ask any questions or even get angry!

19

"Ah, Mia, you're here!" he said with a smile. "Please join us. I don't mind watching your furry friends."

I thanked him and let out a huge sigh of relief. Then I ran over to my classmates.

"Everyone, welcome to Flying 101!" Professor Wingum said as he scratched a big black Great Dane behind the ears. "Today's lesson is the wind tunnel."

In the center of the room was a long, clear glass cylinder with a steel frame. Professor Wingum walked over to it and pushed a round white button on the control panel. The vents at the top, bottom, and sides of the tunnel instantly turned on.

"Your mission is to fly against the wind. This helps build core strength," Professor Wingum began. "Since this is a beginner-level class, there are no obstacles. But it *is* timed. If you take too long, an alarm will go off. The key is to stay focused and balanced while keeping a steady speed."

I looked around to see if any of my peers looked as nervous as me.

Now, I know flying *sounds* really cool, but it's actually *way* harder than it looks. In my first flying class ever, I was saved by . . . that kid!

"Class, please say hi to Penn Powers!" Professor Wingum announced excitedly. "He'll be showing us how it's done."

I immediately hid behind the tallest
kid in class. The last time I had seen
Penn, I was stuck on a really long rope.
It was *super*-embarrassing.

Penn Powers walked into the tunnel. Everyone watched in awe as he easily flew against the powerful wind. He even did a bunch of fancy flips!

When he came out, he bowed as kids burst into applause.

After that I was glad I was going last. Maybe my nerves would calm down before it was my turn.

Some kids had a hard time and other kids did okay, but no one flew as well as Penn. Soon, it was  my turn. I stepped into the tunnel, and my stomach dropped to the floor. I took a deep breath and closed my eyes. Then I bent down to

push off—when
suddenly, I felt
something soft
brush against
my leg.

"Chaos!" I
yelled as my cat
was swept into
the wind tunnel.
Without thinking, I
jumped in after her.

As we tumbled
through the air, I wondered if this day
could get any worse. And then it did.

Because *all* the dogs jumped in too!

CHAPTER 3

Pawsitively Heroic

So there I was. Trapped in a giant wind tunnel, rolling around with my crazy cat and a pack of adorable dogs.

This was not one of my best moments—that was for sure.

But turns out that there *was* one good thing about all this. Looking at Chaos's scaredy-cat face, I realized that it was up to me to save the day.

I held my arms out in front of me and leaned forward as hard as I could. And it totally worked!

I flew toward Chaos, and before I knew it I was so close that I could almost touch her.

But then someone else grabbed her!

I looked up and saw Penn Powers, holding my cat.

And the thing is, he wasn't just holding Chaos. I watched as Penn started gathering all the floating dogs, too.

He put a bunch of dogs on his back
as he held more in his arms. I could tell
it was too much. Even for him.

"Hey, Penn! Let me help!" I yelled. I may not be great at flying yet, but I knew I was strong. After all, during my PITS placement test, I lifted an elephant *and* a car!

"No, I got it!" he replied. "Just make sure to fly through the exit before your timer goes off!"

"Penn, this is too much weight to handle by yourself!" I tried again.

But he just waved me on and grabbed another dog . . . which was exactly one dog too many! Penn lost his balance and tumbled backward, dropping all the animals.

An alarm blared through the tunnel. I needed to do something NOW.

That's when I remembered Professor Wingum's advice: The key to flying was staying balanced and steady.

I sped over to Chaos. Then I found Pax and linked their paws together.

"Hold on to one another!" I yelled as
I connected more animals, paw by paw.

Soon, all the dogs were lined up,
with Chaos in the front. Penn was over
on the side when I shouted after him.
"Hey, Penn!" I called out. "I'll push from
the back. Can you help too?"

"Got it," he replied, quickly catching on to my plan.

Penn grabbed both of Chaos's paws. With all the strength I had, I pushed us ahead while Penn pulled. And we flew out of the tunnel just as the seconds on the timer went down to zero.

THE NEW MISSION

"Excellent job, Mia!" Professor Wingum cried as a bunch of kids gave me high-fives.

"Class, Mia just showed us what it takes to be a great superhero! She made a plan, acted quickly, and got everyone to safety!"

Professor Wingum gave me two big thumbs-up.

That's when it hit me. I'd been so focused on getting out of the tunnel . . . I didn't realize I was flying!

"I really *flew*!" I exclaimed happily.

"You sure did!" Wingum replied. "Your action in the face of danger helped you overcome your fears! This is known as the superhero instinct—or learning to trust yourself. All of you have it. We just teach you how to listen to it."

Chaos purred happily as she nuzzled against my leg.

"One important thing about trusting yourself is also knowing when to trust *others*, too," Wingum continued as he locked eyes with Penn. "Sometimes, even the greatest superheroes need help. Teamwork was the key to Mia *and* Penn's success."

I gave Penn a quick smile. I was so glad we made it out okay. But he just looked away!

I wondered if I had made a mistake.

"So why are there random dogs here, anyway?" Penn asked, clearly annoyed.

"Oh, they followed my cat and me from the clinic," I explained.

"Ha! Why am I not surprised?" Penn muttered under his breath.

My face grew hot as a few classmates quietly snickered. Immediately, I went from being super-proud to super-embarrassed. I may have helped solve the dog problem, but I had to admit, *I* was the one who brought the dogs in the first place.

"Attention, everyone. Looks like our time is up," Professor Wingum said. "Fantastic job flying today. It's a great start! But for now, you'll all have to *walk* home."

As everyone left, Wingum motioned for Penn and me to stay behind.

"Amazing teamwork today—both of you," he cried. "But I'm afraid the job is only half done. These pooches don't belong here."

"Yes, they don't. These pups were all getting groomed for the Downtown Dog Palooza at the vet," I explained.

"Well, good thing the wind tunnel gave them these amazing blowouts!" Wingum said with a laugh.

I looked over, and he sure was right. They all looked absolutely fabulous!

"Ha! Good luck with getting those dogs back," Penn said with a smirk.

"Oh, no, Penn, you're not off the hook," Professor Wingum corrected. "Returning these pups is the new mission for *both* of you."

CHAOS IN THE COMPASS

Penn and I walked out to the Compass in awkward silence. As I struggled to get Chaos into her carrier, I had a bad feeling this mission was doomed for failure.

Because here's the thing: A pack of rowdy animals isn't easy to control. Especially when they're super *cute*!

"Hey, Mia! You are wasting your time!" Penn yelled as I sped past him.

"But we need to get all the dogs to line up!" I cried. With Chaos's carrier still in my other hand, I rushed over to Pax, who was getting a tummy rub.

"There are just way too many distractions," Penn said.

I looked around the lobby. He was right. Rounding up these curious pups with all these superheroes walking around was going to be difficult.

"Watch and learn," Penn declared.

Then he took a deep breath and put his thumb and pointer finger up against his lips.

FWEE-OOO-WEE!

A loud high-pitched whistle echoed through the halls as a bright blue shiny dome covered the lobby. All the animals immediately sat straight up.

"Now *that* is how you get an animal's attention," Penn said matter-of-factly. "By controlling the sound waves they hear!"

I quietly watched Chaos and the dogs calmly follow Penn's voice. He may not be the easiest person to work with, but he definitely knew his stuff.

"Nice job, Penn," I said "Since the dogs always follow Chaos, I'll take the lead. You should watch from the back."

"No, *I* should go first," Penn argued. "*You* follow *us*."

Penn and I argued back and forth until the front door suddenly slid open . . . and Chaos jumped out again and dashed out the building! And just like earlier, all the dogs ran after her!

This time Penn and I *both* froze in shock.

Oh boy. Chaos was going to be the leader whether we liked it or not.

THE TEAM GETS BIGGER

By the time we ran outside, the dogs and Chaos were long gone. I paced back and forth in a panic when I heard the same noise from earlier.

Oh no! Someone was here, and the PITS door had disappeared!

I quickly hid under my cape, wishing
everything would just *freeze*.

And then . . . everything *did* freeze.

Whoa. I knew I could pause things
with my hands, but this was the first

time it worked with me just thinking about it.

I know we're in a hurry, but since things are on hold, let's back up for a second.

Remember how I said Pax's owner was my best friend?

Well, TA-DA! Here he is!

Please allow me to introduce you to Edison Stein—or Eddie for short.

I don't know what he's doing here, but I should probably unfreeze him and Penn now.

I moved my cape, and thankfully, everything unfroze. I'll really have to figure out how I did that later.

"I—I'm just looking for my . . . dog," Eddie stuttered nervously.

"Eddie, it's okay!" I said calmly. "You're right. Pax *was* here!"

All the color drained from Eddie's face.

"Who are you? How do you know me and my dog?" he asked.

I took a second to think carefully.

Other than my parents, Eddie was the only other person who knew my super-secret. But he had never seen me in my supersuit before!

"Eddie, please don't freak out. But it's me—*Mia*! Or right now, I guess I'm Mia Mayhem!"

Eddie continued to back away.

"Oh, come on. It really *is* me. I can prove it!"

Then I grabbed his hand and gave him our secret handshake. Thankfully, that made Eddie break into a smile.

"Mia—it *is* you! Your suit is SO SUPERCOOL!" he cried.

"Oh, Eddie!" I exclaimed exhaustedly. "Today has been a disaster! And we just lost a bunch of rowdy dogs . . . including Pax!"

"Well, good thing I know exactly where Pax is!" Eddie cried, holding up a tracker that he built. Eddie was really smart and always liked tinkering with things.

"Perfect!" I cried happily. "Since Pax loves other dogs, once we find him—"

"We'll find them all!" Penn piped in excitedly.

Eddie looked over his shoulder in shock. He'd been so caught off guard by me that he hadn't noticed there was another superhero right next to him!

"Very pleased to meet you, Eddie. My name is Penn Powers!" Penn said as they shook hands. "Now let's go save those pups!"

CHAPTER
7

FLYING!
OR ... SORT OF

The tracker led us to Eddie's house. We didn't know if Pax was inside, but Eddie waved at us to follow him.

"Um, Eddie," I said, "if your parents are home, we can't just walk into your house like this!"

"Oh right," he replied with a laugh. "Okay, wait here. I'll check for the dogs."

I nodded as Penn started pacing back and forth.

"Which room is Eddie's?" he asked. Penn did not like waiting around. After all, he was a superhero. And he needed to take charge.

I pointed to Eddie's open window.

"We're wasting too much time. I'm going in," Penn declared.

"No, that's really not a good idea," I said as calmly as possible.

"Don't worry. I can check this whole place in a flash!" Penn bragged. Then he took a few steps back, pushed off, and flew into Eddie's room!

UGH. Working with this kid sure wasn't easy. But now that we were a team, there was only one thing to do.

I flew through the open window and tumbled right into Eddie, who was gathering extra leashes and treats.

"Yikes!" Eddie cried. "You said you were going to wait outside!"

"Oh, I know, but *someone* was getting antsy," I said as I shot Penn a sharp look.

"Well, the dogs aren't here," said Eddie. "But I thought we could use some supplies for when we *do* find them."

"Great idea, Eddie!" I exclaimed.

Penn studied the room, and then he said, "Hey! That's a pretty good idea. What does your tracker say?"

Eddie held it up and gave it a wave. "The dogs are on the move!"

"Then so are we!" said Penn, and he flew out the window.

I shrugged. "I think he's really excited about finding the dogs."

"Yeah, I can see that," said Eddie. "I'll get my bike and meet you outside."

ZING!

I flew back through the window, and a few minutes later, Eddie was out on his mountain bike.

"According to my tracker, they're headed across town!" Eddie declared.

"To cover the most area, let's split up," Penn suggested.

For once, Penn and I agreed on a plan. So we lifted into the air as Eddie raced away on his bike.

As I glided along weightlessly, I was so relieved. Flying outside was actually totally AWESOME! Especially because the horrible feeling I usually got in my stomach was gone too!

But then I looked down . . . and that big knot in my stomach came back.

The next thing I knew, I lost control and almost crashed into a bird! As I took a turn, I flew through an open

office building instead, and somehow I created a huge paper tornado! Luckily, no one saw me, and there was an exit on the other side.

But this time, there was only one place for me to go: straight into a giant tree!

CRASH!

"Oh, Mia! Are you okay?" Penn asked as he rushed to my side.

I nodded as I picked leaves from my hair. "I don't think I can do this, Penn," I whispered.

"Well, I think you can," he said with a smile. "Remember what we learned in class?"

"Stay balanced and steady," I replied slowly.

Penn reached down, grabbed my hands, and helped me up.

Now, here's something I wish I'd known before we left: Flying in the real world isn't the same as flying in a wind tunnel. There are a lot of unexpected things you've got to look out for. But the good news is I learned that when a friend is right next to you, even your biggest fears can disappear.

CHAPTER 8

SPRINKLES

THE DOG CHASE

EDDIE'S WILD RIDE

Penn and I zoomed across town. The wind rushing against my face was like nothing I'd ever felt before. The knot in my stomach finally disappeared, and I was able to really look around.

We passed the post office, the movie theater, and even my favorite ice-cream shop! From up above, everything I knew so well looked completely different.

When I dove a bit lower, I saw
Eddie racing down the street. He easily
hopped over a curb, pedaled down a
slanted pipe, and skidded past a row of
trash cans.

But then he started to go down a random alley, and I knew he was in trouble. His tracker must have misled him . . . because he was heading straight into a construction site!

"Look out!" I yelled over the booming noise of giant vehicles.

Luckily, Eddie heard me just in time. He sped over a mountain of dirt, jumped a set of steel frames, and dodged a huge puddle of wet cement.

I was so relieved that Eddie was safe . . . but then I heard him scream.

"AHHHHH!" Eddie cried as a crane hook caught him!

"Don't worry, Eddie!" I yelled as I went into another dive.

I swooped down and grabbed Eddie without his bike. Then I looked over and saw that Penn had caught it.

Whew! What a close call!

I'm so glad I've gotten used to flying because it looks like even great bike riders could use a pair of superheroes.

CHAPTER
9

THE FINAL DESTINATION

Back on the ground I gave Eddie a huge hug. "Maybe keep your eyes on the road next time?" I suggested.

He nodded as Penn came flying down with the bike. Right then the alarm on the tracker started going off. "Let's find these dogs already," said Penn. "I've got to get home soon. Even superheroes can't be late for dinner."

We huddled around Eddie's device
and looked at the map. The red target
was heading east, toward one of my
favorite places in town.

"Hey! I know where they're going!" I yelled. "The park!"

It was all beginning to make sense. Remember how my cat, Chaos, was leading the pack of dogs? And remember how I said that most cats like to lay in the sun? My cat does too. But here's the thing: While most cats like to do that from a window, Chaos likes to actually lay outside.

And if she's outside, the park is her go-to place because, well, there's lots of sun, plenty of things to scratch, *and* a big playground!

Now that we had a location, it was time to get back off the ground. We decided to meet at the fountain in the park. Eddie handed us the leashes and treats.

"You'll get there before me, so I think you'll need these," he said.

Penn took the bag and nodded. "Thanks, Eddie."

Then Penn and I lifted up into the sky.

At the park, I let out a sigh of relief. Pax, Chaos, and the other dogs were really there! The park had been set up for the Downtown Dog Palooza tomorrow . . . and the dogs were running through *everything*!

They raced through tents, knocked over all the chairs, and dug through trophy boxes. I spotted one bulldog chewing on a WELCOME banner while a poodle got tangled up in a pile of streamers.

If we didn't do something fast, the dog show would be ruined!

Luckily for Penn and me, there were no people in sight. We just needed to get things under control before anyone saw us!

So we took the leashes and treats
and started flying around. But as
expected, a pack of hyper dogs (and
a cat) is *way* too much
mayhem—even
for a team of two
superheroes!

That's when I looked over and locked eyes with Penn. "It's time to use your special trick!" I told him.

Penn nodded and lifted two fingers to his lips.

But just as he took a deep breath, a loud whistle that sounded nothing like Penn's echoed from behind us.

THE
DREAM TEAM

When I turned around to see who it was, my jaw dropped to the floor. It was my dad! And unlike Eddie, my dad had seen me in my supersuit before, so he knew it was me.

I started to wave to Dad, but then I stopped. I realized I was in danger of breaking a major PITS superhero rule! Unless absolutely necessary, it was important to keep our secret identities under wraps. And if I wasn't careful, Penn could figure out who I was!

I looked around in a panic, but thankfully, Eddie rode up on his bike, and my dad played it cool.

"Hi, Eddie, it's good to see you," my dad said. "I have been looking for this pack of dogs all day! I never thought they would head to the park. Good thing that they're all safe."

"Well, these dogs escaped from the PI—I mean, we've been trying to get them back to you!" I said before Eddie could reply. I laughed nervously as my dad lifted an eyebrow.

Oh man. I definitely had some explaining to do when I got home.

But luckily my dad knew exactly what to say.

"Oh my goodness! Thank you for tracking them," my dad replied. "But I could use some help cleaning this up. The setup crew from the clinic already went home."

"You got it, sir!" I replied with an awkward salute. I shot Eddie a look as he struggled to hold in his laughter.

Then we split into two teams with a bunch of the dogs. Eddie and Penn fixed the chairs while my dad and I retrieved banners that had blown into the trees. Then we grabbed the streamers and secured them back onto the stage.

Once we finished, everything looked as good as new.

And the funny thing is that after all that mayhem, the animals were suddenly on their best behavior! So Penn and Eddie easily secured the leashes while I led Chaos inside her carrier.

After my dad secured the last dog collar, he stood up and turned to us.

"Thanks so much, Eddie, and um—" my dad began.

"Penn Powers, sir!" Penn said.

"And Mia Mayhem," I added proudly.

Then the two of us flew off as Eddie and my dad walked the dogs, and Chaos, back to the clinic.

The next day at the Downtown Dog Palooza, I walked through all the different stations with Chaos. There were events for best dressed, best ball fetcher, and even best water-skier!

When I stopped by the pool that was set up for water-skiing, I saw that Pax had won first place!

I opened the carrier to celebrate . . . but Chaos had struck again!

I ran around, frantically calling her name. Thankfully, this time, I found her sleeping under a tree!

So you know how I said that most cats like taking naps? Well, I guess Chaos does too.

And before she wakes up, here are
a few things I've learned: For starters,
saving the day takes a lot of work. And
I couldn't have done it alone.

But the good thing is, thanks to the most epic adventure across town, I, Mia Mayhem, can really FLY!

And I guess the craziest and most obvious lesson of all is that I *really* need to fix this good ole cat carrier!

DON'T MISS MIA MAYHEM'S NEXT ADVENTURE!

Oh boy. We're totally going to lose this soccer game.

Seriously, it's *not* looking good. At this point, I doubt we'll be able to make a comeback before time runs out. If by some miracle we do score a goal, *I* definitely need to stay out of it.

Excerpt from *Mia Mayhem vs. the Super Bully*

Why? Because here's the thing: The last time I was on this pitch, I kicked the ball so hard that I accidentally broke the goalpost in half!

Crazy, right? I know. Weird things happen to me all the time. In fact, all my life I thought I was a super-klutz . . . because no matter how hard I tried to avoid it I always caused a lot of mayhem.

But here's the kicker: I found out that I'm *not* a super-klutz . . . I'm actually just SUPER!

Like for real!

I. Mia Macarooney. Am. A. Superhero!

Ever since I found out, I've had to juggle a lot. During the day, I go to Normal Elementary School. But as soon as the school bell rings, I head off to the Program for In Training Superheroes aka the PITS. And at the PITS, I go by MIA MAYHEM!

It's been a crazy ride, so I'm glad that some things haven't changed. Like getting to play soccer with my friends. But now that I'm in the middle of a game we're about to lose, I have no idea what to do. Especially because my best friend, Eddie, is about to pass the ball . . . to me!

Excerpt from *Mia Mayhem vs. the Super Bully*